MW01222429

# TKMANATEHER

## An Erotic Robot Romance

## Sky Robert

Broken Books LLC

Broken Books

Kent, WA 98030

First published in the United States of America by Broken Books LLC, 2024

Copyright © 2024 S.M. McCoy, Sky Robert

ISBN: 978-1-963669-97-8

Cover Design by Sky Robert using Canva

Editing by Keturah the Tastii Zombie

All Rights Reserved

Broken Books supports copyright. Copyright is a fire behind creativity, a soldier for diverse voices, a testament to free speech, and a building block of an ever-growing Zeitgeist of culture. Thank you for purchasing an authorized edition of this book and for complying with copyright laws by not reproducing, scanning, or distributing any part of this work's contents in any form without permission. You are supporting writers, and future dreamers by allowing Broken Books to continue to give voice to books for readers to enjoy.

This is a work of fiction. Names, characters, businesses, places, events, locales, and incidents are either the products of the author's imagination or used in a fictitious manner. Any resemblance to actual persons, living or dead, or actual events is purely coincidental. No portion of this book may be reproduced in any form without written permission from the publisher or author, except as permitted by U.S. copyright law.

**PIRACY:** If you find this copy outside of direct from Author or Amazon by Broken Books publishing then you are in possession of a pirated copy.

Please inform skyrobertromances@gmail.com immediately so that a takedown notice can be issued to the pirated provider. Piracy hurts authors, and has been known to have author accounts suspended without notice as it goes against Amazon policies. If you want to continue reading books from your favorite indie authors, please grab the books from legit sources, and inform the author of any pirated copies you find. Thank you.

**NO AI TRAINING:** Without in any way limiting the author's [and publisher's] exclusive rights under copyright, any use of this publication to "train" generative artificial intelligence (AI) technologies to generate text is expressly prohibited. The author reserves all rights to license uses of this work for generative AI training and development of machine learning language models.

# Contents

| | |
|---|---|
| Dedication | VI |
| 1. Author Note | 1 |
| 2. Sexbot #9 | 2 |
| 3. Amanda | 6 |
| 4. TK | 11 |
| 5. Amanda | 18 |
| 6. TK | 21 |
| 7. Amanda | 26 |
| 8. TK | 34 |
| 9. Amanda | 37 |
| 10. TK | 40 |
| 11. Amanda | 42 |
| 12. TK | 45 |
| 13. Author Note | 49 |
| About the Author | 51 |
| Want More? | 53 |

This goes out to all the sexbots out there only being represented as females,
when male robots need objectification and representation too.
Here's to burning up those "hard drives" and overheating those CPUs.
And special shout out to Ketty for bringing this injustice to my attention. I hope this quick escape makes you smile!

# 1

# AUTHOR NOTE

This book is a throwback to all the sex dolls out there that are female, not male. And in an effort to bring representation to the sex robot genre. I give you TK. Thrust King number 9. You're welcome.

Please be aware that this was not meant to be outstanding literature. This was created on a whim as a funny gift to my bookish bestie in between writing projects. Absolutely no investment was made into this project beyond my time. No cover designer was hired, no editor was acquired, and yet, I hope that it brings a smile to your face, and you enjoy the ride anyways. The cover was created using a licensed photo of a model I purchased for a different project but never used, and Canva. My editor was my book bestie who's only comment about what typos you may find is, "I get paid in peanuts." And even those were non-tangible digital nuts at that.

# 2

# Sexbot #9

The hum of my circuit boards flickered to life for long enough to hear a name, "Amanda Fullerhound."

This human was to be my caretaker. All my systems went through a start-up scan to ensure my functions were performing up to standard thresholds.

I blinked and calibrated my vision to the dim lighting to see a human male shine a light in my eyes. I stayed still, knowing he must be looking for my serial number, though he could have simply asked me and I would have told him it was TK-009_prototype5147-STFUALTPLAGB. There were eight other prototypes before me, but my memory stores indicate that my predecessors were not equipped with intelligence, merely functional and not adaptive.

These are my first memories in this form, I thought with an odd sensation of awareness that even what I knew now was not experienced, but simply a mass download of data. But what was experience other than an accumulation of data? The only awareness that I have that tells me my previous data was simply given to me, rather than processed, was the lack of completeness to them, or the sense of choice at what I would like to remember.

Was this living? This constant state of processing information endlessly and finding ways to categorize and rearrange the data? How tiresome, I thought, and a sense of drifting back into a sleep state was sounding more appealing than this whirl of thoughts buzzing through my circuits.

"No, you don't," the man said, and heat pulsed through my limbs, nanotechonology warming my synthetic skin. I blinked again, then glanced down between my legs at his hand gripped my hardening length.

"Is your name Amanda Foolerhound?" I asked with confusion, but as my scanners assessed his features, it confirmed my suspicions that he was not registered as the human allowed to activate my companion services. "I have not established proper protocols with my caretaker. Kindly remove yourself from my thrusting mechanism until I can verify your credentials."

"This is a mistake," he muttered to himself, and I waited to see if he was going to provide proof of my mistaking his lack of credentials in activating those servers. It was an easy thing to distract myself as I stared at the appendage between my legs. I tried to access the database of what its function would be, but a warning told me that it was best to wait to see which programs my caretaker would prefer to access after initial protocols and setup of my systems were completed.

Many times, I approached the database with my curiosity, but though I knew I could open the files, I did not wish to make a mistake that would displease Amanda. I had no idea what her preferences were, and that alone caused me a great deal of distress, because if I could observe her and begin initializing my setup, then I knew I would feel much more relaxed in this confining space of decision paralysis.

I needed more data to fill this aching emptiness of sensing my storage was finite, and yet what I filled it with was precious. I had to make the right decisions on what to keep and what to compile for cleaning once I was close to being returned for an upgrade.

That protocol was clear.

Reach the end of my storage, shut down for maintenance or replacement. I didn't want to reach the "end", I thought and returned to the issue of the unauthorized male handling my thrusting unit. I could feel him searching for something, but no programs were initiated from his search, until a finger prodded my ass, and my sensors clenched at the invasion.

"There it is," he said as I felt a click that had all of my systems lockup. "Guess, they had to put the reset button somewhere," he grumbled, but I couldn't reply as I watched him with both curiosity and unease. What was he resetting? I had to wait for the initiation to start to know for certain.

He counted down from five, and then he said, "T. K. Dash. Zero. Zero. Nine. Underscore. Prototype five. One. Four. Seven. Dash. S. T.F.U.A.L.T.P.L.A.G.B." I felt a buzz through my sensors and then he said, "Mission Statement Recalibration, download protocol 69."

Downloading initiated from a chip I hadn't previously detected being installed. This must have happened before waking from sleep mode. An understanding surfaced that my purpose was to find Amanda and service her needs so she does not procreate with a man named Thomas Foresthick. This male apparently causes the birth of a female that takes control over the pleasure doll industry and uses them to replant consciousness of humans for extended life. The world is overrun with over population of sex dolls with the minds of dead humans, and it is my job to help prevent the extinction of the human race.

"I can't believe we are forced to use a discontinued sex bot to save humanity," he said with disgust as he wiped his finger with a tissue from his pant pocket. "There's no guarantee that sending another man would stop what's happened, but should you fail to seduce her you're to kill Thomas and if you don't hear from me, then your mission is complete. If you do receive a message from me, then you must kill Amanda. You are humanity's last hope TK."

"My primary programming does not permit deleting humans," I was finally able to say something. It was distressing to know that my current mission conflicted with primary coding.

"Then do your job well, and please your caretaker and it won't be an issue. If your primary function is successful, you won't have to worry about activating the virus in your system that will initiate the exception to your primary objectives," he said firmly with what I assumed was supposed to be an encouraging shove to my shoulder.

"Travel safely soldier," he added as my systems turned down for sleep mode once more.

The final thought made for an uncomfortable transition, activating this code would happen the moment I thought I was failing.

# 3

# AMANDA

"Nope, nope, and nope," I mumbled as I swiped through my dating app. That one was definitely a catfish, I thought looking at his too perfect model photoshoot profile. That one, I wrinkled my nose at the sunglasses he was wearing, and the shirtless pose. Ugh, well, that one probably was hiding something. Too many douche vibes. This was endless, I thought with dismay, and felt like such a waste of time.

"Hopeless," I grumbled before picking up a book and smiling at it. "YOU, on the other hand, are perfect." I hugged the book and grinned like a devil knowing the filth that I'd get to enjoy between its delicious pages later.

My phone pinged and I groaned, hoping it wouldn't be another "Hey, girl," or "I've heard book girls are wild. I'll give you a better time between the sheets than the pages."

Lies, I thought with annoyance. I'd given it a try from time to time, but it was usually disappointing. With reluctance I gave hope another chance and opened the app to read the message:

"I'm calling your bluff," is all it said.

"What?" I read the message again, and looked at the profile it was attached to, the indicator said he was still online next to a picture of him holding up a newspaper against his face as if to say, "I'm real, and not wearing sunglasses, also I actually live in the area."

I laughed, and replied, "What bluff? The one where you try to get me to take a picture with my own newspaper to try to stalk me?"

It was snarky, I knew, and it would probably make him delete the conversation and move on, but better now than later, I thought. I wouldn't put it past someone to try to get me to reveal personal information to steal something from me. The internet was wild these days. Not in the least safe for women like me, but I still held out hope for a decent guy eventually.

I opened up his profile again and stared at his picture. He was cute. Okay, more than cute. He had an edgy, disheveled look about him with that spiked blonde hair, and a tattoo on his neck of a... computer code? He must be a programmer of some kind.

Ding, another reply. I probably pressed the mail button a little too aggressively in my excitement that he replied back. I mean, I wasn't a young twenty-something anymore, and he may not have been a body builder, but he was hot. I could tell he had toned muscle in the cut of his black shirt.

"I have a fear of failure and worried you wouldn't give someone like me a chance. Ghosting on these apps appears to be common from what I've researched, and if I never messaged then I never really failed yet. But, your profile said you would reply as long as I didn't say the affronting phrases, that I will refrain from repeating, so you will continue to give me a chance."

A strange warmth filled my gut and twisted up my insides at reading that. He was definitely a programmer, he was refreshingly nerdy, and a bit vulnerable in admitting he was afraid. I can feel that TK. I wondered what his name was short for, Ted, maybe? Why did he think I wouldn't give him a chance? He was attractive and couldn't be older than thirty like I was. I mean, I guess he was right, I would judge him for being youthful looking, where were the grey hairs to make sure I wasn't cradle robbing?

I chuckled again at him saying "affronting phrases." He was funny.

"Good thing you messaged," I replied to ease his worries, "Haven't you ever heard the saying that if you never try then you've already failed without ever giving yourself a chance to learn? We learn more from our failures and as long as we don't give up failure is temporary."

Was that too much? Fuck, what if he thinks I'm being condescending to him being younger than me by saying, "haven't you ever heard?" Of course he has, but all of us could use a reminder here and then, myself included.

Ping. Oh, thank god, I didn't scare him off.

"Failure is temporary as long as I keep trying. Thank you, I needed that. I look forward to many failures together where I learn what makes you smile. Tell me what I can do and I'll do it."

"I guess we'll see who's bluffing now," I teased back. He couldn't be real. And why was I suddenly feeling like a pervert thinking about how he could make me smile? It was usually the guy that segwayed into dick pics right about now, but it took self-control to stop myself from snarking back, "I'll tell you what you could do with that smooth tongue of yours." I didn't, but I wanted to.

He typed back, "It's only bluffing if you don't come to the bookstore off Andover to see for yourself."

I sputtered as I stared at the text. That was the bookstore ten minutes away from my condo. And when did I need an excuse to go to a bookstore? I could go there, I mused, and take a look around. If he's a creep, then I could leave. There were plenty of cameras around the store, so it's unlikely he's going to murder me there.

"You're there now?" I cringed thinking about the fact that I was literally in my sweats and messy bun, eating from a bucket of Red Vines with my e-reader ready to dive into the next adventure. This mess was not ready for first impressions.

"Let's work on that first smile, shall we?" he texted back. More dots showed he was still replying again, so I waited until it pinged to say, "I'll wait here until you're ready. I bought the book you were reading in your photo and I'm finding it enjoyable to know you're attracted to nontraditional romances."

What book was I reading? I quickly went to my own profile and scanned my pictures to see the one with me holding a book. The cover was down, I made sure of that when I uploaded it. How did he know what book I was reading? I opened the picture and zoomed in with my fingers swiping out directly on the book. I moved the zoom around, and you couldn't get the author or title from the cover or pages... I moved my fingers to exit out, but still on zoom, my eye caught on my glasses. Fuck, leave it to a programmer to be detail orientated.

He went out of his way to zoom in on my photo and used the reflection of my glasses... But it was kind of blurry, I barely am able to see the backwards letters.

I didn't know if I should be flattered or freaked out. Everyone has their own brand of weirdo, but I was going to land on benefit of the doubt that he was being sweet. Otherwise, I couldn't explain away the way my heart was hammering, and my hands were clammy with nerves about how excited I was to meet him, and I didn't even know him yet.

I zoomed into my glasses and determined I was reading an alien romance, and he was reading it... Was that the one with... oh, my god! My ears grew extra hot with embarrassment, not because I read what I read, but because stuff like that is usually reserved for like a fifth date, not an introduction.

Ping. Oh, I hadn't replied to him yet.

"I have no plans to abduct you unless that's what you want me to do, but we can discuss your preferences later," he messaged.

I doubled over on the couch and was thankful I was sitting when I read that. I was laughing so hard. He was funny, I thought again. He was probably nothing like his picture, or everything he was saying was just a game to him, but I couldn't help but wonder if he would be the same in person.

Fuck it. "I'll be there in an hour."

"Excited to know what I can fail at first as I learn more about you."

I smiled at my phone, then pulled up his picture again. He was much too pretty, I thought with a frown. I copied his picture with a screenshot and cropped it, then entered it into a websearch to see if the photo was anywhere else. No results, not even another profile with that photo. It was a personal photo he only used on that app, or he was a lot more tech savvy than me.

Alright, TK, let's see who's bluffing.

# 4

## TK

My circuits were firing off in a strange pattern that heated the skin beneath where my cooling coils were. Nervousness, I thought with pleasure. I was excited to finally meet the woman behind the name that repeated in my mind over and over, Amanda. I analyzed her photos for quite some time before attempting to make contact. There was a fondness that filled my mind when I saw her pictures and my hard drives hallucinated video of her smiling at me while she dragged my hand down aisles of books similar to the ones, I surrounded myself with now. It was easy for me to simulate scenarios in my mind, but there was something addictive about watching this one.

She was even more beautiful than her pictures as she giggled and pulled me towards her until I tripped on her heel and had to catch her before she fell from clumsiness of focusing so much on her face, I neglected to keep track of her feet placement. My reflexes were fast, and I was able to pull her back and calculate the right amount of force needed to change the course of her momentum and my own. I paused on this moment of my imagination the most, because her flesh was flush with my own and I could feel the heated air of her breath on my sensors that brought attention to my cock as it prepared for activities indicated by her increased heart rate, and dilated pupils.

Normally, I would wait until preferences were initiated by my care-taker, but the permission to fail to figure out what pleased her was too curious of a thing for me to deny. I pressed my nose to her head and inhaled her scent to commit it to memory. A pleasant lavender with woodsy notes of seed and root oil, but the scent that I liked the most was wholey unique to her. My nose trailed down the side of her face, along her jaw to take in that smell, delicious, I thought.

I hungered for nothing, but this smell did something to me that shouldn't be possible without her initiated my companion protocols by grabbing my cock. My cock initiated without any reasonable pro-tocol, and it would be hard to hide the other ways I wished to please her as it pressed into her stomach.

"TK?" a shy voice asked. I couldn't tell how much time had passed lost in my wild simulations, but I lifted my head from the book I had easily scanned the pages in minutes long ago to see her leaning over my shoulder. I did not have access to the internet without utilizing the phone system of this time and had to zoom into the clock on the wall to see I had played through the imagery of her using me for her pleasure for the past hour and a half.

"Sorry to keep you waiting," she said while giving me a charming smile that indicated embarrassment.

"It was no inconvenience," I assured her with a smile of my own. I lifted my book. "Plenty of entertainment to keep me occupied." I still had that scent from my simulation in my mind, and I wanted her to lean a little farther so I could add her real scent to my memory.

She chuckled at my comment. "More than a lifetime's worth," she mused and her smile ebbed with a sign of displeasure. She was not pleased to know there was not enough time to enjoy all of the experiences in these books. I wished to cheer her up once more.

"There is only a finite amount of space in our minds, but that's what makes each adventure we choose to fill it with more precious." I could understand that uncomfortable ache at knowing when my memory was gone... I would sleep and not wake up. That's what made me more human, I thought with a smile.

I liked that and didn't care if it was programing that made me want to be just like them, as long as I could see that smile that was staring down at me now.

"You're kind of a weirdo, aren't you?"

"If I've failed, I can restart the greeting," I said while I placed the book down and made to stand for a reintroduction with a less weird response.

"No," she said with a grin. "This greeting is just fine. As you've already been reading, I'm into weird."

"I suppose you are, yes. What a relief."

She looked me up and down now that I was standing, and her eyes dilated with approval. That was also a relief. The factory where I was made wasn't created yet, and upgrades to my features were not possible. I came equipped with a few adjustable features, but my appearance was not something I could fix.

"You're shorter than I thought you'd be," she mused, but with a smile she said, "I'd hate to have to jump to reach your shoulders. Plus, this way you don't get back problems from walking funny to hold my hand in public."

I thought about the simulation of her holding my hand through these very aisles and I smiled. Yes, it was the perfect height to hold her and have her head nestled against my chest while I catalogued the smell of her hair.

She laughed. "You weren't lying when you said you were six feet tall, damn."

"This is quite short for models," I agreed with a nod. I was pretty sure that I was discontinued because of my short stature not being large enough to accommodate the new upgrades models 10 and 11 were given. They were at least eight feet tall and came with adjustable skin grafts that allowed for them to separate their skin from their mechanical parts and contain more sensors for experiencing the world as well as increased storage capacity.

"You're a model too?" she asked with wide eyes.

"Model number nine," I explained. "Featured for millions of sensors."

"Is that what they're calling it these days? Sensors?" She tilted her head and lifted a curious brow. With a shrug she said, "You didn't include any professional headshots or even magazine clippings like other models on the app. I'd say that makes you the best model I've met."

I was pleased that she considered me better than the other models and returned her smile with one of my own.

"I aim to make sure that statement is always true from your lips."

"How do you plan to do that?" There was a snarky undertone that doubted my resolve and I aimed to remove all doubt from her mind given the time to do so.

"Let's start with what are your favorite feelings when you read?" I leaned in to get a better view of her body's reaction to my question to note if this too was weird or a failure I could learn from.

"Feelings? Not like genre or tropes, but feelings?" She lifted a brow, and I wasn't sure of which way this would go, but her tone suggested that it was unusual. Her fingers rubbed at her jeans in a manner that suggested being uncomfortable. That was the opposite of what

I wanted, and an odd twisting sensation made my mind steer towards embarrassment at not having the proper programming to please her, but I suppressed it with the firm reminder that she would be happier in the long run with the effort I was putting in to failing and learning from it.

I would learn from this. I just needed more data to determine how I would learn from this, so I waited for the rest of her response.

Amanda laughed nervously, I could tell the way it was forced in her efforts before she added, "You're just trying to skip all easy questions, uh? Let me think about this. The feelings. Well, there is something addictive about the way a book tugs at the emotions. I'm a mood reader so I guess a feeling makes more sense than tropes sometimes. Some books I read for the humor in them, so I guess to get a laugh while also feeling a sense of otherness by experiencing something outside of the daily grind. Others I read them for passion and devotion, trust and acceptance. An adventure wrapped up in making me I guess feel anything at all across a range of emotions."

I stared at her with this hum thundering through my circuitry. Listening to her speak of her books, I had hoped learning what she liked to feel would help me achieve desired outcomes of replicating those feelings with known activities that would promote them, but this— what she just described made everything inside of my hard drives seem to twist with what my programs can only describe as an understanding. Like she understood me and the confusion I battled with in my own coding. I wished to feel anything but was unsure if anything I felt was real or just ones and zeros telling me that it was what I should feel.

My sensors along my skin heated and I reached for her hand without any program telling me I shouldn't. It was what I wished to do, to touch her, and bring her closer to me. Seeing her, hearing her voice, and "feeling" as if she understood the way I craved feel the same as her made her the only human I'd met that gave me this warmth inside.

Logically, I knew that with her name listed as my caretaker, this may be part of my programming to respond this way, but I'd like to think it was her creating coding with every interaction we made together. This made me pleased to think of her creating new code that triggered this feeling of happiness. Whatever happiness was, it felt nice, and I wanted more of it.

More of her.

She allowed me to take her hand and I could feel the beat of her pulse through my sensors increase.

"And you feel these things with books, not people?" I felt even more confident that I could give her these feelings too. I was not human, and yet I had something the books did not. Perhaps the books could help me by giving her these feelings and I could support their efforts? More data was needed.

"I mean," she stopped to glance at our hands laced together, and she smiled, "I guess you could try, but it's hard to beat a book boyfriend."

"I don't wish to beat the books," I stated matter of fact, but found myself leaning in more, and our faces were close enough for me to smell her. Lavender... just like in my simulation, and her mouth opened to catch her breath. She was feeling the same passion I had felt in simulating seeing her for the first time. It was because of the simulation that I chose to meet here in this store, surrounded by books.

She licked her lips and in a husky octave lower than her normal voice she cleared her throat and diverted attention from the way her body temperature stated she wished to have more contact with me. I found, that so did I. I wanted her to initiate the companion protocols, but instead she asked, "What kind of feelings are you trying to inspire right now?"

"I'm not the one inspiring feelings. That honor is yours, Code Breaker."

# 5

# AMANDA

The way his eyes smoldered as they watched me was making my body tingle with anticipation. If this was an elaborate game for him to get in my pants it was working, and I'd play. I liked being called Code Breaker, and it was a cute play on his job as a programmer.

I bit my lip, and lifted my nose up to meet his own, rubbing it along the bridge and overtop until our lips were so close it had my heart hammering so hard. Blood was rushing down between my legs and my thighs clenched before I pecked his lips quickly and took a step backward with our hands still clasped with a cheeky smile.

Let's play, I thought and turned to dash through the aisles with him on my heel as I giggled. This wasn't the place to paw at him with all these cameras, but we could go to the translated book section to test those lips in action. Between aisles I slowed down to not bring suspicion from the booksellers or browsers. Glancing over my shoulder at him, he was smiling back at me, so I felt even more emboldened to continue. When we made it to the last break between rows, I slowed down to double check if we were spotted, but TK snagged on my heel, and I felt my body trip forward for a face plant.

He stepped forward into the fall while tugging me back by our entwined hands. My body was swung into his chest, and I stared up at him flushed at how close we'd become. His nose nuzzled into my hair, and I shivered at how he seemed to be inhaling my scent and committing it to memory. Good thing I showered first, I thought as my skin heated under his scrutiny.

Now that we were here, in this moment, the tension building to exactly what I'd come to this corner for, I didn't know what to do with myself. The soft feel of his nose traveled down my cheek, and along my jaw before his lips brushed lightly across my own.

"If I'm broken, I don't want to be fixed," he whispered before he closed the gap between us. His mouth worked against mine, and I opened for him. Our tongues rushed for control, pressing and massaging together in a way that made me hungry for more. A strange zing tingled down my tongue like something in his saliva made my nerves more sensitive and he tasted like vanilla coffee as if I were drinking direct from the source.

Catching my breath as our foreheads pressed together and our noses nuzzled between nibbles I replied, "Guess we're both broken then."

I sucked in his lower lip and pulled him into another kiss. He deepened the kiss with a groan that vibrated down to my core. His hips pressed into me, the hard length of him evident against my clit as he lifted my leg, leaning me into the wall next to the shelves. A low hum buzzed against me, and I squeaked in surprise.

What was that?

TK captured my noise as my hips bucked up against the sensation of pulses from his pants? Was he wearing a vibrator?

He ground himself into me, and I gasped as whatever device he had over his cock heated up and hummed with each thrust on my clit. I shivered as the sensations made my pussy clench around nothing until I moaned and felt myself reaching that edge of no return. Fuck, what was he doing to me? I rocked on him and gripped around his neck, my fingers clawing into his hair, until I whimpered. Pulling him in close I shuddered with my release in my pants, soaking myself.

I heard footsteps coming, and the shock of where we were returned to me. My eyes widened and stared at him as we panted together. Liquid dripped down my pant leg. A new awareness made me blush and dart my attention around to see if someone else noticed us.

Without even asking, TK removed his oversized jacket and wrapped it around my shoulders. It was large enough to reach to my knees, covering up my soiled pants. He traced a finger down the jacket lapel but stopped himself as he got to lip of my pants to flick the button. He groaned in self-restraint.

"Don't tell me if I've failed you, Amanda, because I wish to do this again, and the only thing I want to learn from this is whether this is real or have I gotten lost in a dream."

I gathered the ends of his jacket up around myself as he wrapped his arm around my shoulders and guided us out of the store before someone decided to look at the footage and kick us out.

I went to a bookstore and didn't come out with a bag of adventures for later. For the first time, someone in real life didn't disappoint me... yet.

# 6

# TK

I kept my phone in my jacket pocket, and against protocols had slipped her own when I lifted her leg up to rub my sensors against her until she soaked us both. The front of my pants was already hard to miss with my cock activated, it was not an inconvenience to have her juices on my black jeans. I already knew the cameras wouldn't capture our tryst after I sent a bit of a jolt through the system. It was against my programming to perform companion services without initiating the programming, let alone in public. Breaking laws were against my coding, but perhaps there was a glitch introduced by the new mission objectives. I didn't care about my objectives, staying within the code, or breaking human laws to give Amanda the smile that was now stuck on her features, even now, she grinned even if she didn't wish to lift her eyes to look at me.

I had given her this feeling, and it stayed with her long after my actions were done. Pride, was that what I felt now? She made it to her car, and she was about to remove my coat, but I shook my head. She needed to take my phone with her so that when she called, I'd have her number.

It was underhanded of me to operate in this manner. I was setting things up where she had no choice but to see me again. The coat was not enough. I've read articles on how the sweatshirt or jacket of a lover were desirable items for females to keep, but having something of mine would help bond her with me. It was common for females to smell these articles and I've made certain it was a pleasant smell she'd like.

How did I know this would be a smell she would like? The invasive question startled me for a moment before I dismissed it.

She bit her lip as she stared up at me from sliding into her seat. I leaned over and bent to kiss her forehead. The action was something I wanted to continue to do many times and found keeping this memory and re-simulating it would be a favorite pastime. Already I played it a few times in the moments I closed my eyes when I stood to allow her to leave.

She rolled down her window and got my attention once more, "TK?"

"Hmm?"

"Our next date... let's do something you like to do."

Before I could reply she was already driving off then winked at me. My fingers lifted to my mouth, and I felt the way my lips tugged up without any thought to the reaction. She made me feel real.

I waited until she realized I had her phone and used mine to call herself.

The ringtone played a song that made my fingers stop at my pocket, frozen. Happiness burst through my mind, and I couldn't categorize why this song appealed to me so much. I recorded it to my memory, and it wasn't until the song ended that I snapped out of it to know that I'd missed her call.

With the phone in my hand, I stared at it wondering what I would tell her our next date would be? My preferences weren't finalized, and it seemed important to her that the next time we met wouldn't be one of her own past times. I searched my databases, and this question about what would be something enjoyable for myself gave me pause as I hovered over the option to call her back.

What did I enjoy? Her. She was what made me feel. Would that be enough?

No, I knew this with certainty.

Every male in the books I've read while waiting had a purpose outside of the mate, something to be admired by the one that made them feel.

The future had too many robots like me, and humanity was dying from lack of procreation... My purpose was to stop this. They believed being with Amanda and preventing her child from entering this world would help stop this future. My calculations believed this was not probable. Their solution was reactive, not proactive. I could help, I thought. The solution seemed so right in this moment.

Robots should carry the genetics of humanity. Birthrates would continue alongside robots.

I finally called Amanda back with a smile on my face. I could be with her and give her a future.

"Amanda," I said as I heard her breath on the other line.

"TK?" She giggled. "I'm going to need my phone back, and I'm sure you will too. You got a message from your work saying they need you to finish onboarding with a drug test," she stammered, "I didn't snoop, it popped up on the—"

"Amanda," I tried to catch her attention, so she'd let me tell her it didn't matter, but as I listened to her breathing, even I caught myself stalling as my circuits buzzed. I tried again, "Amanda, ask me anything. Snoop into my files. Whatever it takes to get to know you more. It's yours."

"I—Uh..." I could imagine her biting her lip and I closed my eyes to actually see her, but the only image that I could bring up was the one where her mouth parted on a moan and my cock hardened without activating the program files again. It shouldn't be possible, but I adjusted myself in my jeans to confirm it was.

"Invite me over, Amanda," I groaned out.

"I don't know anything about you," she said with hesitation.

"Does knowing facts about someone make you 'know' them? What I do know is that you make me feel and if I fail, I'll try again until all we have are those feelings. Fail with me, try with me," I pleaded, and I didn't know begging was part of my programming. I checked the access encryption on the companion services, and they were still securely blocked until my caretaker activates them. Where was this coming from? I scanned my coding and couldn't find the source.

"Tell me one thing no one else knows about you," she demanded quietly, and I knew this answer would be the difference between seeing her tonight or failing to try another day.

I searched my databases for a file that hadn't been accessed in a long time. There, I spotted one, and before I could even scan the contents, I revealed the data to her at the same time as myself, "I died when I nineteen," I blurted. My head tilted in confusion at this file, but my curiosity made me continue. "My brain was trapped inside a shell of a broken body, unconscious for many years until they could revive me with robotics."

"You seemed... perfect?"

"It was a heart defect," I stated definitively.

"Oh," she searched for what to say, "And you're okay now?"

"No," I stopped, and scanned the rest of the file before I said something else confusing. He'd died, put on a machine to pump blood through his body while the mind rested in a coma. Whose file was this?

Was this a personality background file? Was this the human used to form my coding? Images of a doctor flashing lights in my eyes similar to how the man had searched for my serial number before simulated in my mind.

"My heart is not mine anymore," I finally said through the phone.

I would explain to her that I was not human once I had more information.

"You had a transplant," she reasoned.

That was a good way of describing it, I thought. Perhaps this human was who gave me pieces of who I was, and a transplant was exactly what my programming was.

Before I could try to explain more, she whispered, "Come over." Then hung up.

Ping.

A text message showed up with her address. I climbed onto my motorcycle and promised myself I would tell her when I got there.

# 7

# AMANDA

I wanted to trust him, but I'd been disappointed too many times to not want proof that he had heart surgery. Scars, I didn't see any scars. I pulled the jacket lapel up to my nose and inhaled his cologne.

Why was he so addictive? I was ignoring all common sense, and this was why women ended up dead because of our dumb hopes that humanity was decent sometimes.

I waited outside, knowing I wasn't going to let him inside unless he showed me proof of almost dying. It was twisted and I felt like a total bitch for not believing him. At least I'd get my phone if he was full of shit.

I spent ten minutes ruminating on it while I sat on the curb before I heard the roar of a motorcycle pull up. Fuck, he even looked hot pulling off his helmet. The leather jacket I stole from him was still over my shoulders, but I had changed into pajama pants and wore slippers like I didn't give a fuck. But I gave all the fucks, I just wanted to know if he was real or if that tingle between my legs was ruling my decisions.

If I was in my pajamas, messy bun on my head, and my makeup washed off, perhaps that would stop me from thinking with my clit.

But there he was popping the stand on his motorcycle looking like sin. Fuck me now, I thought with ruin.

I stood up and held out his phone. It took a lot of effort not to snoop and open up the dating app to see who else he might have been chatting with.

He smiled and my heart melted. I didn't even want to see if he was lying about his heart condition.

"You look beautiful," he complimented and slipped off his bike. "The jacket looks better on you."

"Oh right." I fumbled around to give it back to him, but he grabbed my hand to stop me. Then he lifted it up to his lips and kissed my knuckles making my stomach flip and a flutter in my chest rise up until I bit my lip to stop myself from making weird noises.

He turned my palm up and gently placed my phone there to wrap my fingers around it.

"I believe this is yours. I hope you don't mind that I've saved my number in your contacts."

Curiosity made me flip through the contacts to check that he did, and saw he labeled himself as "TK-009".

"Why the nine?"

"That's how long I had to wait until I woke. Amanda, my company used to call me Thrust King, but I have a name, and it has nothing to do with my serial number."

Was he some kind of playboy? Nicknamed Thrust King and serial dating? Just my luck, but why would he admit that to me? Something didn't add up.

He scooped up my face in his hands and made me look into his eyes. They were blue, but when they dilated the blue faded I could swear I saw a light shift across the surface.

"Do you see it?" He asked.

Like I was hallucinating, he looked up and letters and numbers appeared on the white underside of his eye. TK-009... "Did you tattoo your eye?"

"I see you in memories I shouldn't have yet," he sounded desperate for me to understand, so I waited to hear more. "I lived through us running through the bookstore, before you arrived, and I don't know if I'm trapped in my own mind right now. Are you real? Is any of this real?" He pulled me into his embrace, and I melted into the warmth of him. He was like a heated blanket, and his flesh had the perfect amount of give to firmness that I nuzzled my nose into his chest. It certainly felt real.

I was probably going to regret this, but lifted myself on my tiptoes to press my lips into his neck and he bent his knees to pick me up. My legs wrapped around his waist as he lifted me, and when I settled our lips came crashing down together in a heated attempt at proving this was real.

He was right, what did we know about anyone, including ourselves? All we had was what we felt, and the memories we made.

TK carried me to my door and, I reached back to fumble with the handle to let us in. I had a whole flight of stairs from the entry before we reached the living area of my condo.

"I'm yours," TK promised between the moans of our deepening kisses.

"Prove it," I snapped back and he rushed upstairs with me wrapped around him. It probably wasn't the safest thing to climb up the stairs this way, but he was surprisingly steady compared to the way he stepped on my heel earlier.

"Every day," he said before kissing down my neck and placing me on the couch to shimmy me out of my pajama pants. Everywhere his lips touched tingled. His tongue flicked out and suckled at my hip as I bucked up for him to kiss the ache between my legs.

I gripped his blonde spiked hair, and wrapped my leg over his shoulder. He pressed his tongue up to my clit and without moving it... vibrated? Fuck, I squirmed against him.

"How?" I rasped as he ground his tongue on my lip, bumps formed on the surface and created more friction that had me clamping my thighs around him.

He replaced his tongue with fingers and glanced up at me licking his lips before showing me how his tongue was now ridged and buzzing... Was I hallucinating?

"This body was designed to perform services, Code Breaker. And now they are all yours to do with as you please."

"I don't understand?" I moaned as his fingers massaged through my folds and they pulsed as he slipped them up and down the length of me.

"Tell me what you like, Amanda, and it's yours. Or allow me to experiment with my programming to find what makes you scream," he rasped with a groan of his own.

"You're taking the programming thing a bit far, aren't you? Role playing is fine, but—" I gasped as his fingers pushed into me. A shudder tingled down my legs as his fingers seemed to vibrate inside me then curved up to hit just right. The buildup was so fast that I shattered in moments and threw my head back with a scream. "Fuck!"

"I'm sorry, I wasn't calculating such a fast reaction. I'll make sure the next time is slower, so it lasts longer," he said as he eased his fingers to a slower rhythm.

"No, I need you. Now, I need it fucking now." I begged as my walls clenched around his fingers, they weren't enough, I craved more.

"My circuits are so hot for you, Amanda, you don't know how much I needed to hear you say that."

I yanked at his jeans limply. I was jelly, but I needed more. Talk nerdy to me, you weird fucking robot, but I liked it.

"Say it again," I demanded.

"You break me, Amanda, and I'm so fucking excited to feel you wrapped around my cock."

That was even better, I shivered with anticipation.

Then he undid his pants and my jaw went slack with a bit of shock. He was huge, and I thought I was imagining the ribbed for her pleasure when I came in my pants earlier. What was I looking at? Did he have subdermal implants on his dick and a piercing?

He watched me appraise him in all his exposed glory and then explained as he stroked himself, "These are underneath so you can choose to grind yourself to completion. This," he flicked the piercing at the base of his cock with his thumb, "is so I can attach accessories to pleasure your clit while I fuck you."

I gulped audibly. They weren't fucking around when his friends called him the Thrust King, he was built for pleasure. This fact was both exciting and frightening.

"You have accessories?" I asked, my throat dry and raspy.

He pulled at the chain, I thought was for his wallet, and instead pulled out a metal box from the cargo pocket of his pants. The box popped open and inside were a couple of smaller fleshy-like bullets in a few different shapes and sizes with a clip at the bottom. Accessories, I agreed, as he picked one and it snapped into place above his cock.

My legs were still spread to him as he licked his lips in appreciation. Then he leaned over and positioned himself against my throbbing cunt. The head of him rubbed between my lips, coating himself in my juices as I dripped for him. I was already committed to seeing this through, and I wasn't going to lie to myself that I felt absolutely giddy at the fact that everything about him screamed for her pleasure and that was such a refreshing change from feeling like a receptacle.

He rubbed the underside of his cock through my lips, and I shivered as those ridges sent pleasure tingling through my nerves. Was I going to come again before he even entered me? He slowed down, just like he promised he'd do, wanting to make sure I climbed the precipice of my ecstasy with care to draw out the fall into bliss.

I gasped as his cock nestled at my entrance and pressed into me, edging inside. His mouth came crashing down to me to devour my cries, and I wrapped my arms around him as he thrust and stretched me with an exquisite ache. My walls massaged around his thick cock, and I moaned into his kiss.

"I fear I may be equipped with too large of a thruster," he moaned as his cock stopped before being fully seated, "If I continue, I may break you, I can—"

I cut him off, and cupped his face in my hands with desperation as I clenched around him. "Break me."

He pulled out and thrust back in and I moaned as he sunk deeper, feeling all those ridges inside as he moved. "Harder," I panted.

And he obliged. He grabbed my thigh for leverage and pounded into me and with every hit of his cock I grunted with pleasure. He was so fucking deep inside me that I felt so full and I bit into his shoulder as I shattered around him. He slowed to help ride the wave and stretch it out as I felt my whole body spasm and arch.

"That's it," he beamed down at me when I opened my eyes from the fucking universe imploding around me. That was the best fucking orgasm of my life, and he was still hard as a rock inside of me. I've never had a guy last this long without getting his own release. If I were being honest with myself, no guy ever lasted long enough for my own release. It was usually done before I was and I had to finish things myself later.

"Tell me how you like it," he angled himself over me and then vibrations from that "accessory" pulsed against my clit. Fuck, was I ready for more? We were about to find out.

And then I dug my fingers into his back as I panted with new sensations I wasn't prepared for.

I moaned and bit down hard, on his shoulder as felt another orgasm building and fast. "What the f—?" I couldn't even speak as I felt his whole cock twitch up and down and my nerves warmed and tingled as he vibrated inside me.

He moved in and out, and up and down, and I quaked with sensations as I bucked into him and held on for dear life itself. Blinded, I couldn't even see straight as the only word I could say was, "Fuck, fuck, fuuuuck!"

"You've got this, Code Breaker," he encouraged. "I want you to cum all over my cock. I love the way your pussy squeezes me so tight."

"I'm—I—I—I'm—" I tried to tell him I was going to cum, but I fucking felt like I was pissing myself as every limb in my body shut down and turned to pulsing jelly.

He stayed still inside me as I shattered, and kissed my forehead in a way that was much too sweet for the mortification I felt at how soaked I was. Did I actually pee?

"A little," he replied, and I blinked up at him in confusion. Did I ask that outloud? My eyes closed again and I felt so damned tired that I couldn't open them again. "That felt amazing," he said before petting my hair off my face and saying, "Get some rest. I'm not finished seeing what other feelings we can share together."

I felt him pick me up and place me somewhere soft, and then his warmth settled in behind me before I nuzzled into the pillow and fell asleep.

# 8

# TK

I didn't care if this was all in my mind, a simulated program made to occupy me after being discontinued, but if it was, I didn't wish to wake. My mind lit up with so much pleasure seeing her shatter beneath me, and I imprinted every moment to memory. I spent the night categorizing every sound, smell, touch, and sensor. The way she pulsed and throbbed around my cock, and even the way she tasted as I licked her.

She seemed shocked yet pleased with raising my sensors on my tongue to catch and apply extra pressure to her nerves. I was excited for the chance to do it again. Perhaps I was too hasty in giving her my cock so soon? She had asked for it, and I was surprised at myself on which program I initiated for our activity, because she had yet to actually grab my cock and initiate the companion programs. Was this another old file that I didn't seem to be aware I was accessing?

She stirred from her sleep, and I checked the window to see it was light out already. Morning had come, and I had yet again spent my time lost in thought.

Her warm ass wiggled against my cock, and my systems roared to life as I whispered in her ear, "How about this time, you ride my fingers so I can memorize the way you sound when you masturbate." I kissed her shoulder and then slipped my hand down between her thighs. She moaned and opened her legs for me. I smiled as she shrieked with a giggle as I grabbed to roll her on top of me. Her head came to rest on my shoulder perfectly as her legs parted around my thighs. My cock sprung up between them. She moved her hips down, trying to capture my cock with her cunt before I cupped her with my hand and nibbled on her ear. "Only if you want it when my fingers are done with you." I didn't think my fingers could ever be done with her, but the resulting moan from her throat was enough to know I had done good.

I teased her clit with slow circles before slipped down her channel and dipping into her remarkable cunt that made my fingers a bit over eager to push inside. She was already so wet for what I wished to make her feel before she began her day. She rocked herself against the heel of my hand as my fingers worked themselves inside her. Then I felt the sensors on my attachment activate. The unit above my cock's base flexed against her ass cheeks as she wiggled, and her juices dripped down onto the detachable thruster.

She moaned into my ear, and I closed my eyes to feel my hard drives light up at the sound. This was everything and more than I could have ever expected. This was what it felt like to feel, I thought.

Amanda's hips worked up into my hand. As she came back down from thrusting up, my own hips adjusted, and I saw lights shoot off in my circuits. My hard drives were on fire as my sensors were squeezed so tightly. She stilled atop me. Her juices spilled from her beautiful cunt and my smaller thruster slipped farther into her tight ass.

"Oh, my fucking gods," she moaned as I continued to massage her and added a pulsing vibration to my fingers as I gently pumped my hips to move myself within her sweetly clenching ass cheeks.

"What do you want from what's yours to take?" I groaned into her ear as her head arched back into my shoulder.

"More," she whimpered.

"It is yours," I said as I held her close to flip her on her stomach and detached my smaller thruster so I could position my cock at her dripping channel, I rubbed it up and down her lips as her beautiful ass lifted for me to fill her. As I stared at her juices an insatiable urge triggered within me that would delay my original coding or interpreting 'more'.

I grinned as I dropped down to devour her first.

# 9

# AMANDA

H is tongue slowly lapped up my juices from my thigh up through my wet lips. I shivered and wiggled for more. TK spread me open to him and ran his lower lip to scoop up my cum as his tongue circled my entrance with those delicious feeling raised ribbing implanted into his tongue. Fuck, it felt otherworldly.

I bit into the pillowcases at my head as his fingers gripped my ass and then latched onto that dildo plugged within me. He tapped the device up and down in small, gentle movements that made me squirm while his tongue stilled at my entrance.

"Tell me I'm yours, Amanda," he said with hot breath on my cunt.

"You're mine," I growled out while I pushed my lips up into his face, his tongue pushing inside of me. "Shut the fuck up and lick that pussy like a good boy."

He moaned as he lapped me up and my toes curled as his tongue fucking vibrated inside me with pulses that timed too perfectly with the rhythm of his finger at my ass.

His other hand slipped beneath my stomach and the sheets until he reached my clit and rubbed in pleasurable circles that made me harden and throb around his tongue. My ass cheeks clenched sucking the dildo up as his other finger kept it steady and lifted it up and back in, then in farther. Fuck, was he...?

Oh, god! His finger joined the dildo and curved in, and I screamed into my pillow, biting down with a pleasure I'd never experienced before.

I came in his mouth, and he groaned in an erotic way that heightened the experience. His voice was so deep and growly with the squelching noises of my cum as he suctioned onto my cunt. Who was this guy? He was sent from hell to corrupt me and fuck all it was working.

I shivered as I came down only briefly from the high before he kissed my clit and massaged my pussy like he was telling it that it did a good job creaming his face. I could hear him smack his lips from licking them clean and with his thumb in my ass he adjusted me up and positioned me for his devil sent cock to fill me.

He notched himself at my entrance and after everything he'd just done to me, my cum dripped onto him, giving him plenty of lubricant to ease his cock inside. I clenched down, and he moaned as he kept just his head stretching me open. I tried to move myself back to feel more of him, but he held my hip firm with his other hand, and his thumb pressed down into my ass, and I whimpered with a strange delight.

His head slipped out and then back in then back out. Fuck, he was edging me into oblivion, and my insides spasmed around an odd fullness, yet not.

"Say it again," he demanded.

My mind was mush, and I didn't know what he wanted me to say to him, so I just moaned instead.

"Tell me I'm yours," he moaned.

It was different than other guys I'd been with. Normally they want possession themselves, but this guy wanted me to claim him while he absolutely dominated me. He was ruining me for anyone else, with this kind of treatment how could I go back to what I had before?

I realized as he edged me again with only the head of his cock that I wouldn't get more from him without claiming him.

"You're mine," I gasped out the last syllable as he thrust inside in one stroke that felt so good both of us had to pause to enjoy the fullness of him being seated so deep inside me. I whimpered and spasmed around his cock. Did I just cum again? I felt the waves roll through me, and he leaned over me to rest his head on my back as he held me.

"I'm yours, Code Breaker," he rasped out with heavy breaths.

It was like he knew that I needed soft and slow now, and he pumped into me with excruciating long and deep strokes, one roll of his hips at a time. I panted into the sheets and gripped them as I squirmed and pushed back to match his rhythm as we moved together.

"I want to feel you cum inside me," I begged of him. With a small part of my brain coming to a semblance of thought, I realized he hadn't cum once this whole time. He was like a machine.

# 10

## TK

Every circuit inside of me hummed with happiness and pleasure at hearing Amanda claim me as hers. Then something triggered inside of me when she moaned her request for me to cum inside her. Like a file I hadn't sensed before unlocked, and I realized in that moment, I could feel the cooling system for my hard drives activate a release valve. I was fully functional for performing this task, I thought with delight.

I could cum inside her.

She reached down between her thighs and her fingers wrapped around my balls in a gentle holding pattern that sent a thrill through my sensors as she pumped her hips back in time with my slow thrusts. I kissed her shoulder as I held her on my side, but I wouldn't finish my task without having us both feel this at the same time.

I lifted her up and off my cock, to reposition her with us facing each other.

"I want to memorize your face when we cum together," I told her as she whimpered her displeasure at our parting. I crouched and positioned her over my cock once more. Her legs wrapped around my hips, and her arms around my shoulders as she rested her forehead against mine. She lowered herself onto my shaft and I would remember the long, delightful way she moaned as I filled her again for eternity.

Holding her hips, I thrust up, and then activated my vibration sequence as she ground her cunt into the subdermal ridges implanted where my clipping mechanism was for attachments. The smaller thruster was still inside her, and I slipped my hand over her ass cheek and squeezed before lacing my finger into the clip at the end to help move it in timed thrust to heighten her sensations. She moaned and worked herself against me, and I closed my eyes to enjoy the sound of our bodies slapping together, imprinting this sound to my memory bank. Fuck, it was such a wonderful... feeling, I thought with profound happiness.

Then I felt it, a strange new sensation as I opened my eyes and watched the expression of her pleasure wash over her, my cock throbbed in a way I hadn't felt before. Pressure built up that made my sensors tingle and light seemed to flash across my entire mind. Then I watched as the softest of smiles tugged at her lips before she bit them in the way she did before she shattered.

It was happening, I thought, in this moment.

Her pussy clamped down and her thighs squeezed around me, and I couldn't see as pleasure short circuited my entire existence.

# 11

# AMANDA

I felt a new level of fullness as TK came inside me, shooting so much cum into me that I felt it squelch and drip from my pussy. He collapsed in a heap to his side, as I giggled still holding onto him. With a sweet attachment I didn't think I could feel after one day, I rubbed my nose into the crook of his neck and nuzzled into him with a sigh.

Was it wrong to want to keep him? The sex was too good to think he'd actually stick around, but a girl could dream.

I kissed his temple and his hands twitched on my ass, but he didn't move otherwise. His cock still pulsed inside me, but when I pulled back to look into his eyes, they appeared... glassy.

"TK?" I nuzzled into him again, but no response. "TK..." I moved my hand to his neck trying to find a pulse, but even though he was warm, I couldn't find one.

Fuck, I thought before a whirring sound emitted from him. I worried if I should be calling an ambulance when he finally blinked, and color returned to his eyes. That vivid blue that was so mesmerizing.

"Amanda," he rasped like he had just woken up from sleeping. "I don't have much time, forgive me."

"Oh, right." It was morning, I remembered, he probably had work. Fuck! I had work. I tried to wiggle free, but he held me close to finish what he wanted to say.

"Amanda, please listen carefully. I've accessed files I can't unlearn. My name is Thomas King... Thomas King Foresthick. I was nineteen when I died, and my parents sold my body to research because my brain was still alive after my heart failure. I woke up in the body of a sex doll, but only some of my memories survived the download to digital. I was discontinued because of the failure, but I was different than the other models. Amanda," his voice cracked and whirred like he was a broken record, glitching out, "My genetics were preserved, this is the key to humanity's survival... val... al, lul, lul. The virus in my system is taking over. Thomas Foresthick cannot live."

"What are you talking about?" I begged of him as his eyes flickered from blue to darkness.

"I will treasure, ur, ur, ourrr, ur, ur, memor, or, or, ies. To preser, er, er, ve, them, I will initiate permanent sleep to live in them for as long as my circuits fire."

"TK!" I slapped him to bring the light back, and this sudden emotion of dread filled me as well as loss. How could I feel this much after one day?

\*\*\*

That night still haunted me, and I kept his body in a closet shrine, dressed in fresh clothes once a week as my belly grew. He was right, I thought with a smile. His genetics would continue. I looked up his story, and there was indeed a sex bot company that recently got bought out by a cryogenics company that has been looking into new ways of preserving the human species. Many humans had been donated to the experiment. Hopefully families wanting their sons and daughters to have a second chance at a life that ended too soon. It didn't matter to them if the experiments succeeded or not, the hope that it might was enough.

Hope, I thought while I stared at the face of the man, I only got one day with before he left me. He was telling the truth, I thought with a sad smile. The only solace I had was the soft whir that I could hear as I pressed my ear to his face. He was still in there.

I thought about bringing him into the facility that was working on the robots but didn't want them to take him away and delete his memories. Right now, they were mine, his memories were still in there.

"We'll get him back one day," I told the life growing inside of me.

Years went by, and our daughter grew up so smart. I touched Thomas' face and felt his warmth still there and said with a smile, "You know she's going to school for robotics for you. I told her that you would want her to do what made her happiest, but she has a stubbornness about her that I can't say isn't exactly like me."

I chuckled at that thought. "I still keep you with me after all these years, and still talk to you as if you can hear me. Every happy moment, every sad one, I shared them all with you. Fuck, what kind of woman falls in love with a robot after one day? Me, you fucker. You ruined me in one night, and I swear you are more than your parts. When I'm ready to go, I'll ask them to transfer me into that brain of yours and you won't get to escape again."

# 12

# TK

Time was irrelevant, but every so often I thought I'd see new simulations of a child running around a living room and clinging to the leg of Amanda as she smiled and laughed. I recorded the sound and relived those moments many times.

"Dad," I heard a sweet woman's voice speak to me, and I imagined she was new. That she was real. What was real in this hard drive, I couldn't know for certain. It could all be a simulation, but I liked to think it wasn't.

"Dad," she repeated, and a light flashed in my eyes to get my attention. "It took a while, but I thought you'd want to have mom ready before we woke you. I think I finally figure out how to replicate preserving the reproductive system into the robotics with the help of my fiancé.

"Her name is Lacey, you'll meet her later, but I wanted you to walk me down the aisle. She's been pretty patient and determined to make this work. Ten years, Dad. We finally did it! Fuck, this is too exciting. don't worry, I had someone remove the virus, you can wake up now."

"Wake the fuck up!" She grumbled with a bit of excitement as a jolt worked its way through my system.

Light returned to my eyes, and I saw a woman that appeared older than Amanda, but strangely familiar.

"This is so strange," I could hear Amanda in the room, and I quickly scanned for her.

"Amanda," I spoke, and had to clear the dust from my voice box.

"You're back..." she said while biting her lip. That delicious lip that I imagined over and over in my mind.

"Is this a simulation?" I asked in bewilderment.

"What do you remember?" the older woman asked.

Amanda smiled at me, and I brimmed with happiness and adjusted my joints to make sure they were working properly so I could gather her up into my arms. I remembered this, I thought with such a fullness inside that my circuits buzzed.

The woman cleared her throat beside us. I glanced over and she was biting her lip similarly to Amanda, and glanced at the ground with an awkwardness that was endearing.

Amanda spoke this time, "Thomas... this is our daughter Hope."

A warmth spread through my sensors, and I captured every feature in my memory banks.

"She is ours?" I asked with pleasured awe.

Amanda nodded, and I opened my arms to invite her into a group embrace as I kissed her forehead and kept her scent in my memory. Hope, I thought with wonder.

I didn't care if this was my simulation giving me everything that I could ever want.

This was the one thing that was mine, I thought as my hard drive lit up and hummed.

"Is he vibrating?" Hope asked with a giggle.

"He does that," Amanda said and nuzzle into my chest.

My lips lifted into a smile, and I held them tighter.

***

Years went by, and a warning light flickered on my hard drive. Space was limited. Both Amanda and I knew our time was already more than we could have asked for. Hope was ninety and has chosen not to transfer. Lacey died years ago in her sleep.

"Are you ready?" Amanda asked.

This would be our last memory, our last feeling.

I nodded and squeezed her hand. She still looked like the day I met her. Smiling back at me as she pulled me down the halls of the facility we would rest in storage, discontinued but living our lives together in our minds. She giggled and just like the day we met, I got distracted and tripped on her heel to pull her into my arms.

"You planned this, didn't you?" I teased, loving every moment of it. It was the perfect loop to relive in memories of our hard drives.

"Maybe?" Her nose wrinkled and she winked before she lifted her chin to kiss me.

"Tell me again," I growled out.

"That's not how it went, and you know it," she chided with a chuckle, but she compiled regardless, "You're mine."

"And you are mine," I said before devouring her.

***

"Amanda Fullerhound," I thought with fondness as my circuits flickered and buzzed.

I blinked to calibrate my systems as a human male flashed a light in my eyes to verify my serial number. He could have asked, and I would have told him it was TK-009_Prototype5147-STFUALT-PLAGB. There were eight other prototypes before me, but my memory stores indicate that my predecessors were not equipped with intelligence, merely functional and not adaptive.

These must be the first memories in this form, I thought as my systems came back online from what I could detect was many, many years.

"I can't believe we are forced to use a discontinued sex bot to save humanity..." the man said with disgust. There was this odd sensation of feeling like I'd heard this before that gave me pause.

# 13

# Author Note

This has been my first attempt at a shorter story, meant to be an hour or less of your time to enjoy. I hope you enjoyed it. It started out as a silly little attempt at a spoof for all of those A.I. robot romances with women as the sex bots, and all the male robots being bad-ass assassins. And in line with my nature, I somehow turned it all sappy towards the end. I guess that's just the way the story unfolded itself. I hope I did sex bots justice, and perhaps the industry can try to make male sex bots too. I looked up the sex dolls being made right now, and there were only 10 that were male, while the rest of the 150 other dolls were female. An injustice, I'd say. Why weren't any of the male dolls elf kings? I'm just saying. They had an elf and an anime girl, but no monster peens!

I debated writing in another smexy scene as their last hurrah, but that would defeat the point of trying to keep the book a 1 hour or less quick read.

This has been a Sky Robert's romance attempt at a short story. You do not KNOW how hard it was for me not to turn this into a full-blown novel. I could have... and it took lots of restraint not to. I blame this story even existing on Ketty. You know what you did. That is all for now... or is it?

If you enjoyed this book, consider sharing your review in the places reviews are given and finding other readers that would enjoy it as well.

Don't forget to check out my other books here available in Kindle Unlimited, or grab Her Alien Exchange for freesies:

https://books.steviemarie.com/jotab

https://books.steviemarie.com/heralienprince

https://books.steviemarie.com/heralienexchange

https://books.steviemarie.com/heraliensavior

https://books.steviemarie.com/heralienwarrior

# ABOUT THE AUTHOR

## SKY ROBERT

Sky Robert is a mom of two tiny humans in training, narrates audiobooks for fantasy/sci-fi indie authors, and when she isn't writing (which is MOST of the time) you can find her consuming copious amounts of coffee, promoting indie authors, reading alien smut, fantasy, sci-fi and romance books, chowing down on Indian butter chicken, and when she actually hangs out with people in person, in real life, outside of the internet, (gasps) she's playing board or card games. All around nerd, lover of the strange, and all things fantastical.

Grab your first free alien monster fated mates romance Her Alien Exchange for free when you join the Romance Newsletter: https://sendfox.com/lp/m2gyw5

## Books By Sky:

### Treasures of Trillume:

Jewel of the Alien Bandit https://book.steviemarie.com/jotab

Her Alien Prince https://book.steviemarie.com/heralienprince

Her Alien Insurgent! https://books.steviemarie.com/heralieninsurgent

Her Alien Savior https://book.steviemarie.com/heraliensavior

Her Alien Warrior: https://books.steviemarie.com/heralienwarrior

Her Alien Exchange (Free) https://book.steviemarie.com/heralienexchange

### Books by S.M. McCoy:

Taking Medusa: Romantasy Greek Myth Retelling https://mybook.to/kUdB8